THE ALLIANCE

Christians

AND

Aliens

KENNETH WALTER

CHAPTER 1

The Taking

Everything about Joe was ordinary. His income, house, car, and neighborhood were all just average. He was not married in his thirties, was a member of the Christian Church, and worked in a furniture factory.

One morning he awoke with a start.

"Good grief, it's daylight, and I overslept!" He looked at the alarm clock, and it was blank.

"Darn, the power must have gone off last night. I'm going to be late for work! I need to call the boss."

He hurriedly dressed and went into the front room to get his phone. He turned on his phone and it was dead.

He grabbed a quick cold breakfast, then went to the garage to get his car. Of course, the garage door opener was not working, so he had to unlatch it and open the door the old-fashioned way—by lifting it up.

He got in, fastened the safety belt, closed the door, and turned the key. The engine turned over but did not start. He tried it again—same result!

"What the heck is going on?" he exclaimed.

He got out and walked to the front of his house.

There was absolutely no activity, no cars, no people. His neighbor's dog barked at him. *That, too, was strange. He knows me and never barks*, he thought to himself.

While he was standing there trying to understand what was happening, a shadow came over him. He looked up and saw a large circular object overhead.

Suddenly he found himself seated in a circular room about twenty feet in diameter. He was dressed in a one-piece dark-blue uniform and dark-blue shoes. Two tall thin alien beings in light-blue uniforms with large heads and dark oval eyes were seated across from him. *Oh god, help me*, he thought.

The one on his left started talking to him in a high-piercing voice, "We are not going to harm you. I am Number 1. He is Number 2. We have chosen you because you have something special that we need. Others of your kind have been put in a state of suspended animation. They will recover in a few hours. All electrical power grids have been temporarily shut down. Your nation and several others were on the verge of an atomic war. We could not allow that to happen. All computer electronic devices have been rendered inactive to disable atomic bomb missile launchers, and bomber airplanes cannot fly. We have lived here in peace with you for thousands of years. We live in the earth and under the oceans. An atomic war would destroy the earth and every living thing, including us."

"What are you going to do with me?" said Joe with a shallow, shaky voice.

"You humans are symbiotes. You have a physical body with an ethereal entity inside. You call this entity a spirit. Your physical body traits were determined by your parents' DNA. Your spirit was made for you by the Creator God. It was infused in you at the time of conception. You have a strong wise spirit, and you listen to it. We have watched you for some time and decided that you have personality traits and qualities that we need to use. There are others like you whom we have also chosen. You will be with them soon. None of you will be harmed."

CHAPTER 2

The Chosen

Turning to Number 2, he said, "Take us to Rainier Base."

Number 2 turned his seat and a window opened in front of them. Joe could see a blue sky and a few clouds. Suddenly the window went dark and then opened again. Joe could see a large mountain in front of them. It was Mount Rainier in Washington State. *That was a quick trip from North Carolina*, Joe thought to himself.

"Yes, it was," said Number 1. "That is the way we travel."

They were headed straight for the base of the mountain, still going very fast. Joe became worried that they were going to crash into it. But they didn't.

The window went dark again, and a door opened. Number 1 and Number 2 got up from their seats and started toward the door. Number

2 took him by the arm and lifted him up. "Come with us. We will not harm you."

They walked down a ramp to where a silver egg-shaped vehicle was hovering just off the floor. A door opened in it. They got in and sat down. It had five seats. Number 2 took the one up front. Joe and Number 1 took the two behind it. It had no windows, just a soft glow inside for illumination. The door closed when they sat down.

Joe felt a slight bump then the door opened. When they got out, he could see that they were on a platform inside a large auditorium. It was almost filled with others like him seated in rows around the room. Four aliens, all dressed in light-blue uniforms, were seated in a row on the platform in front of them. Number 1 took a seat with them.

Number 2 took him by the hand and led him to a seat in the auditorium by a very attractive woman. She had a worried look on her face. Number 2 then went back to the front platform and joined the others. The vehicle was gone. The woman took his hand and said in a whisper, "I am Ann." Joe whispered his name back to her and gave her hand a gentle squeeze.

A seventh alien entered the platform wearing a bright-white uniform. He stood in front of the others facing those seated in the auditorium.

CHAPTER 3

The Explanation

There Was no podium or microphone. He raised his arms, and the whole auditorium became hushed. He lowered his arms and began speaking.

"I know you are very frightened by what has happened. I assure you that we will not harm you. We respect you because this planet was created for you. We came here a long time ago. We made the same mistake that your nation and other nations were about to make. We had an atomic war, and our planet became uninhabitable, so we had to leave it. Through ages past, we have protected your ancestors from visitors from other planets who wished to harm them. We continue to protect you from these harmful visitors. We have also helped your ancestors by bringing technological advances to improve their living conditions. We hoped that sometime in the future your civilization would become advanced to the point that we could reveal ourselves and be good neighbors with you. Unfortunately that did not happen. All computerized worldwide electronic devices have been made inoperable to prevent nuclear bomb missiles and bomber airplanes from working. Your living conditions are now what they were before computers and cell phones came into use. Devices that do not rely on computers will function. All firearms have been confiscated.

"You here will be the leaders of those not chosen. You will be assembled into groups with those who have compatible personalities. You leaders will be responsible for setting up governing policies for the towns and cities that you will be sent to. Each group will be assigned a representative from one of us on this platform. He will be the communicator to me for your group."

A translucent bubble formed around Joe, Ann, and about ten others. When the bubble opened, they found themselves standing in Union Square, Hickory, North Carolina. They were still dressed in dark-blue uniforms.

CHAPTER 4

Home Again

"This is my hometown!" Joe exclaimed. Several of the others said the same thing. While they were standing there completely dumbfounded, residents from the town began to gather around them. Joe saw several familiar faces. The alien that came with them elevated himself so all could see him. He began speaking in a soft voice, but all could hear him.

"I am Number 5. I will be your connection to Number 1. Those you see in blue uniforms are your new town leaders. You will work with them to decide how you want to organize your city government. They will be the new officials for the various offices. Joe is the new mayor. He was analyzed and found to be the best choice for this position. You all should go to the city hall and have a meeting to start the government reformation."

He then came down to ground level and went over to Joe.

"I am going back to Rainier Base but will keep watching you and the others. If you start getting into trouble, I will come and help you solve it."

"Just a minute!" said Joe. "What is the existing mayor going to say about this?"

"Call a meeting with the existing city officials. I will be there to verify your authority."

A translucent bubble formed around him, and he vanished.

Joe turned to Ann and said, "I would like you to come with me." She smiled and agreed. Bill, Sam, and John came over to him. He had worked with them at the furniture factory. Joe shook their hands and said that he was glad to see them. He asked if they would help him form the new city government. After some conversations, they agreed and started walking to the town hall. The other chosen ones gathered around and walked with them toward the city hall.

Most of the town residents started walking with them. They began shouting at Joe, asking what was happening. Joe turned to them and shouted back. "The aliens mean us no harm and will be helping us. Please calm down and come to the city hall. This new situation we are in will be explained to you."

When they came into the building, Frank, the elected mayor, came up to him and asked what was going on. Joe asked him to bring the other city officials into the meeting room for an explanation.

When they had all gathered in the meeting room, Joe stood up to address them. Number 5 was already there.

Number 5 stood up and began speaking, "We have taken control of your national government. We want a new government to lead the nation in a more peaceful manner. The state, county, and local city governments are to be formed according to guidelines given to them by the new national government. This will take some time. Until these guidelines are established and given, you will form a temporary city government to maintain law and order and to provide for the needs of the city residents. We have appointed Joe as the new mayor."

Frank, the elected mayor, stood up and started to speak; but a blank look came over his face, and he sat back down.

A bubble formed around Number 5, and he disappeared.

Joe stood up and began to speak. "Will the elected city officials please stand and tell me your name and office."

"I am Frank, mayor."

"I am Carl, city manager."

"I am Don, deputy city manager." "I am Ed, assistant city manager."

Joe introduced his friend Bill and asked him to work with Carl.

Joe introduced his friend Sam and asked him to work with Don.

Joe introduced his friend John and asked him to work with Ed.

Bill, Sam, and John agreed to these responsibilities.

Joe said, "I expect you elected officials to work with them and instruct them in how your office functions. They will be my liaisons to you.

The other chosen ones in blue uniforms will help you in any way needed. Are there any questions that need to be addressed at this time?"

There was much grumbling, but no one had anything to say to Joe.

The chosen ones that came with Joe began talking with city officials trying to decide how they were going to work together. John went with Ed, the assistant city manager, to his office. Joe asked the mayor, City Manager Carl, and Deputy City Manager Don to come with him, Bill, and Sam to Don's office. Joe had decided that this office was the one that needed the most work.

CHAPTER 5

Law and Order

J oe asked Bill about any city problems that needed to be addressed.

He said, "We have no communications now that the phones and computers are not working. How are we going to manage the city?"

Joe said, "You have an information technology department. Put them to work on it."

Don said, "But we have another serious problem. We have no firearms or functioning police or fire vehicles. How are we going to maintain law and order? Hickory is mostly a quiet peaceful place to live, but we do have a few troublesome individuals and criminals that come from outside the city to steal cars and rob stores."

Joe replied, "The aliens said older equipment that did not use computers would be functional. We will need to find these old vehicles, repair them, and put them back into service. Your police radios and stun guns will still work, and you have batons and handcuffs. Veterinary stun dart rifles use compressed CO_2, so they will still be available. Amateur radio operators will probably help us contact other cities and the county government.

"There may also be some old civil defense radios and phones that we can use for city officials. Residential phones will be a bigger problem. They will need to be the push button tone type with connecting cables to a central routing station. Some of the old phone cables are probably in place and functional. The central routing station is still there, so it can be put back into service. Antique shops and the museum may have some of the stuff we need. And we can always just write and mail letters. The post office probably still has some of the old delivery trucks. Looks like we have a lot of work to do. Let's get busy and meet back here tomorrow at eight o'clock for progress reports."

CHAPTER 6

Now the Good Part

Joe turned to Ann. "Do you live here in town?" "Yes, I live with my mother, Gail. She needs me to help her. Do you want to come over for dinner?"

"Yes, that would be very nice. I am single and not a very good cook." As they walked, he asked her what she thought about this new situation we are in.

"It is very scary, but I think we can learn to live with it. It will be hard to give up cell phones and computers. It will be like starting a new, more simple life. I think it might even be better without all the distractions we had before."

"I believe you are right about that. I think the furniture factory can make the transition, and I will still have a job when my position as mayor can be given back to Frank."

They drove to a genuinely nice neighborhood. Her mother's house was a two-story brick with an attached garage. When they arrived, they went in to find her mother. She was sitting in the living room, softly crying.

"Mother, this is Joe. He is going to help us." He walked over to her and took her hand.

"Hello, Gail, I am pleased to meet you. I will help you and Ann get through all this terrifying ordeal."

"Thank God! I have been praying that someone would come to help us."

Ann said, "Dad's old car is in the garage. You can check to see if it will run while I get us something to eat. The garage is through the door at the end of the hall. The keys are probably in it."

"Okay, I hope it will run. We sure need it."

Joe found a 1969 Dodge Aspen four-door sedan in the garage. The tires looked good, so he got in. The key was in the ignition. He turned it and got only a click. The gas tank was half full. "Sounds like a dead battery. I hope there is a charger in here." He looked around and found one on a shelf. Opening the hood, he connected the battery to the charger and plugged it into an electrical outlet. He turned the charger on. It started humming and indicated a fifteen-amp charge. He went back into the kitchen to tell Ann the good news. "The old Dodge has a dead battery. I found a charger, and it is charging. It will take several hours, but the car will probably run when the battery is charged up."

"That's great!" she said. "Dinner will be ready in a few minutes."

Joe went in to talk to Gail. "Your husband's old Dodge is just what we need. How are you feeling?"

"I am weak and don't walk very well, but otherwise I am okay." Ann came in from the kitchen and told them that dinner was ready. Joe and Gail went in and sat at the kitchen table. Ann sat down with them, and Gail offered to ask blessing for the food.

"Dear God, we are thankful for this food and ask You to bless it. I am also thankful that You have sent Joe to us. Please give us courage, strength, and ability to get through this difficult time. Amen."

Joe and Ann both said, "Amen."

When they had finished eating Joe said, "Please excuse me. I am going to see if the car will run." He got up and went into the garage. The charger was now reading two amps. *That looks good*, he thought. He disconnected the charger, closed the hood, got in, and turned the ignition key. The engine started turning over but did not start. He tried again, but still no start. He tried again. This time the engine sputtered and started running. "Oh, thank You, God!" he exclaimed. He got out and opened the garage door so he could let it run. He went into the kitchen where Ann and Gail were cleaning up the dishes.

"The car is running. We are going to be okay."

"Oh, thank You, God," said Ann.

Turning to Gail, Joe said, "I need to ask you a favor. My mom and dad live in Charlotte, and I want to see if they are okay. Can I take the car to go see them?"

"Of course you can," she said. "You go ahead and do whatever you need to do."

Joe said, "I will drive over tonight, then come back in the morning to see if you are okay. Do you want me to pick up anything for you?"

Ann said, "We need a few things. I will make a list." She made a quick list of the items needed and gave it to Joe.

"Okay," said Joe, "I will pick them up in Charlotte on my way back here."

He went to the garage. The car was still running. He got in and drove out onto the street. He drove to the freeway and headed for Charlotte.

When he got to his parents' house, he saw the lights were on, and everything looked normal. *That looks good*, he thought. He parked in the driveway, went up to the front door, and rang the doorbell.

His dad said, "Who is there?"

Joe said, "It's me, Joe. I came to see if you are okay."

His dad opened the door. "Oh, I am so glad to see you. We had no news about Hickory, and we were worried about you."

His mother came to the door, gave Joe a big hug, and said, "For heaven's sake, come in and tell us what is going on. Can you stay with us?"

Joe said, "I am glad that you both are well and the situation here is not threatening. I can stay the night but will have to leave early in the morning. I have important work to do in Hickory tomorrow. Let's go sit down so I can tell you what is happening." When they were seated in the living room, Joe told them about the alien takeover and their shutting things down. "They are helping us through these difficult times, and things in general will gradually improve. I think our lives will be better after all the problems are worked out." He asked his dad if his car was working.

He said, "Yes, it is, but most of the neighbors aren't. When I go into town for anything, it is almost deserted. There are a few stores and gas stations open, but items are scarce and there is talk of a food shortage."

His mom said, "It is getting late, and you look very tired. Let's go to bed, and we can talk more in the morning."

The next morning after breakfast, Joe said, "I am the new temporary mayor of Hickory, and there is a lot of work to be done to get the city running again. I have some city associates and friends from the factory that are helping. We also have an alien who we can call on if something comes up that we can't handle. I really need to get back home and see to my new responsibilities, so I will go now. Do you still have the old phone?"

"Yes," said his dad.

Joe said, "It will be working again when the phone lines and routing station are put back in order. I will try calling you in a few weeks, so plug it in and wait for my call. I will fill you in with more details then."

Joe got into the car and drove into town to pick up the items on Ann's list, then he headed back to Hickory. When he arrived at Ann's house, he pulled into the garage. Ann heard him arrive and was waiting at the hall door when he got there. He gave her a hug and handed her the items he had picked up for her. He went in and said hello to Gail. She said, "I am glad to see you and that you made the trip safely."

Joe said, "It is good to see you too." Then he turned to Ann. "Do you want to come into the meeting with me?"

She said, "Yes, if Mom will be okay. Let me ask her."

Gail had heard the conversation and said, "You go ahead with Joe. I will be fine until you get back."

Ann went over to her, gave her a kiss on the cheek, and said, "We will be back this evening and fill you in on what has happened."

When they arrived at the city hall, there was a crowd of people waiting out front. They saw Joe and started shouting at him wanting to know what was happening. He shouted back, "We are working out the details and will let you know more this afternoon." With that, he and Ann walked into the building and went to the meeting room. His friends and the elected officials were there waiting for him.

Joe said, "I am glad you are all here, and I hope you have some progress reports for me."

Sam said, "Don and his crew have found two fire trucks that can be made serviceable, and there are five cars from impound and wrecking yards that can be repaired and painted for police cars."

"That sounds encouraging. How about phones?"

Don said, "The IT group has found twenty-three old phones that are working, and the routing station is being repaired as we speak. We have identified many of the phone lines that are good."

"Excellent!" said Joe. "Distribute the phones so at least one phone is in each neighborhood and city officials all have one."

Don said, "We will need to find more phones, but I think that is possible. The airport is another matter. The tower radar and radios are not working. None of the passenger planes are working, and we have only a few other small planes that will still fly but under visual flight plan only. We did find two civil defense radios that are working. I am not sure how we will use them yet. We contacted two radio amateurs in town, and they agreed to work with us if we need long-distance communication with other cities."

"Excellent," said Joe. "How many people do we have in jail?"

Don said, "We have two at the present time. One for drunk and disorderly conduct and one for domestic abuse."

Joe said, "Okay, let them serve out their time, but for any new violations, I have some ideas for more strict punishment that will make people think twice before doing such things."

Don said, "What do you have in mind?"

Joe said, "Make a modified old English pillory and put it in front of the city hall. A day or two in that, and criminals will reform quickly."

Don said, "Isn't that cruel and unusual punishment?"

Joe said, "Yes, it is, but cruel acts deserve cruel punishment. Let's make a crime and punishment list. It will be posted in front of the city hall beside the pillory. I will make a drawing of the modified pillory design to give to the city mechanics. We still have lots of work to do, so let's adjourn for now and meet again tomorrow morning."

Ann had been sitting beside him throughout the meeting. She was surprised and impressed by his leadership. Joe turned to her and said, "Let's get some lunch. I know a good place to eat."

She agreed, so they got in the car and started driving. Ann said, "I have a degree in design and drafting. I can help you with the pillory drawing. I have a drafting board and drawing tools. After lunch, we can go to my place and get started on it."

Joe said, "That will be a big help." As they were driving to his favorite diner, he saw a homeless man sitting on the curb. "That is completely unacceptable. I wonder how many more like him there are. Let's drive around and look." As they drove up and down city streets, he saw several more. One of them was obviously on drugs. "I need to talk to Don and Sam about this."

After lunch, they drove back to her house and parked in the garage. They went in to find her mother. Ann told her what they were going to do, then they went upstairs to her study. It was a large well-lit room with a drafting table, cabinets, and bookcases. "Tell me what you have in mind for this modern pillory."

"I want it to restrict the prisoner to the location. The person can either sit or stand. It should be made of three-inch-diameter stainless-steel pipe welded to a square base plate with four holes for one-half-inch anchor bolts. The center pipe should be about three feet high with a cover and ring centered on top. The top ring will have a chain attached to a pair of standard handcuffs. The chain should be long enough so the prisoner can have access to a porta potty behind a flat stool close by the pillory."

"Okay," said Ann, "I will get to work on it. I can have the drawing for you by tomorrow morning."

"That will be good. I will come by about seven thirty and pick it up. Do you want to go to the meeting with me?"

"Yes, I would like that."

When they arrived at the city hall, everyone was waiting for them in the meeting room. Joe said, "Looks like everyone is here, so let's get started. Sam, what do you have?"

"Don and I have a draft crime and punishment list. It includes both prison and pillory punishments. It divides crimes into Misdemeanors and Felonies. Pillory punishments will only be applied to misdemeanors committed by adults. Several city councilors do not like pillory time at all. Sam suggested that prostitution should not be a crime. If it were legalized and responsibly managed, this would reduce police arrests and reduce rape and other sex crimes. Nevada is doing well with it. This would need to go to state for implementation."

Joe said, "Good, let's look at the misdemeanors list."

Don put it up on the reader board so all could see it.

Crime	Punishment
Disorderly conduct	18 hours from time of arrest
Disturbing the peace	24 hours
Domestic violence	48 hours
Drug possession (less than 10 mg)	18 hours from time of arrest
DUI	48 hours
Indecent exposure	24 hours
Public intoxication	24 hours
Shoplifting (up to $1,000)	36 hours
Vandalism (up to $1,000)	36 hours

Joe said, "I have a drawing of the pillory. It was made by Ann." He gave it to Don.

Don said, "It looks doable, but I think we should add a poster on the front with the crime printed on it. We will also need security cameras installed so it can be continuously watched on monitors. I will give the drawing to our maintenance shop mechanics for construction. I will also go to the IT department for the installation of the security cameras.

Joe said, "Those are particularly good ideas. Another matter has come to my attention. Ann and I saw several homeless people on the streets. This is an unacceptable situation. We need to have them picked up and sent to the hospital for evaluation."

Don said, "Yes, we know about that. They can be divided into three groups. Poor who cannot afford a place to live, drug addicts who cannot afford both drugs and housing, and those with severe mental problems."

Joe said, "It will be in the best interest of the city to get them off the streets and to provide what they need at city expense. We could set up low-cost housing or apartments for the poor. Drug addicts could be treated at the hospital and severe mental cases committed to a state-run mental hospital. When I told Ann's mother about the mental hospital idea, she said, 'We had those in the '70s. They were called nuthouses, and the state-run ones were all closed by 1980.'"

Several months later, Joe could see that the city was managed well, and many of his suggestions were being implemented. The pillory had very little use and became more of a monument than a functional device.

He told Frank that he wanted to be a private citizen again and resigned as temporary mayor. His friends did the same. He went back to work at his old job in the furniture factory, and things were going well for him.

Joe and Ann became very close. One day as they were walking, he told her that he loved her and asked her to marry him. She said yes, so they were married in a Christian church. Joe sold his house, and they moved in with Ann's mother.

CHAPTER 7

The National Solution

After several years, the states agreed to a national convention according to Article 5 of the United States Constitution. National government responsibilities and limitations were voted on and passed. The states elected a mutually beneficial president and vice president. Other high-level national offices were similarly filled. The original thoughts of the nation's Founding Fathers for the rights and freedoms of its citizens came into being.

All atomic bombs in the world were dismantled. The fissile materials were put in secure bunkers for later conversion into fuel for atomic electrical power plants. Highly radioactive waste from these plants was being vitrified and stored in deep geologic repositories so it could not be used to make "dirty" bombs.

All computerized devices were now functional. All automatic pistols and rifles were destroyed, but six-shot revolvers were permitted for police and personal protection. Five shot-bolt action rifles were permitted for hunting. People all over the world were living peacefully with each other, and life in general was much improved over what it had been before the aliens' takeover.

CHAPTER 8

Now We Can Be Good Neighbors

The supreme alien, dressed in his brilliant white uniform, came on national television, which was broadcast worldwide, and gave the following address.

"I am very pleased with the new world governments that have been established. Your world is now ready for us to be good neighbors. You know of our existence even though you will see little of us or our activities. We will continue to protect you from other nonworld visitors that mean you harm. You will be seeing our cylindrical and spherical drones in your skies that are watching for these harmful visitors. You may also see some fighting in your skies when we must destroy the harmful visitors. I wish you all peace and prosperity."

National presidents and leaders from all over the world then came to their local stations to express gratitude for the peaceful world conditions that were made possible by the aliens.

La Fin

ABOUT THE AUTHOR

Ken Was born and raised in Wyoming. He graduated from the University of Wyoming in 1958.

He was married and enlisted in the Army Medical Corps shortly after graduation from the university. He served three years in Texas at Brook Army Medical Center.

After discharge, he had several technical jobs in Utah, Idaho, and Washington.

He is now retired and living in Washington State.